How to Catch a MOUSE

Philippa Leathers

WALKER BOOKS
AND SUBSIDIARIES
LONDON · BOSTON · SYDNEY · AUCKLAND

This is Clemmie.

Clemmie is a brave, fearsome mouse-catcher.

She is brilliant at stalking and chasing.

She is patient and alert.

She knows everything about
how to catch a mouse.

How to spot

A MOUSE

A

B

C

A .... A whiskery, pointy nose

B .... Two round ears

C .... A long pink tail

Mouse Tracks

scale
cm
0
1
2
3
4
5
6
7
8
9

In fact, Clemmie is such a fearsome mouse-catcher
that she has never even seen a mouse.
All the mice are afraid of me, thinks Clemmie.

But Clemmie is always
on the look-out.

What's that?

A mouse has a long pink tail ...

but this is not a mouse.

There are no mice in *this* house!

What's that?

A mouse has two round ears ...

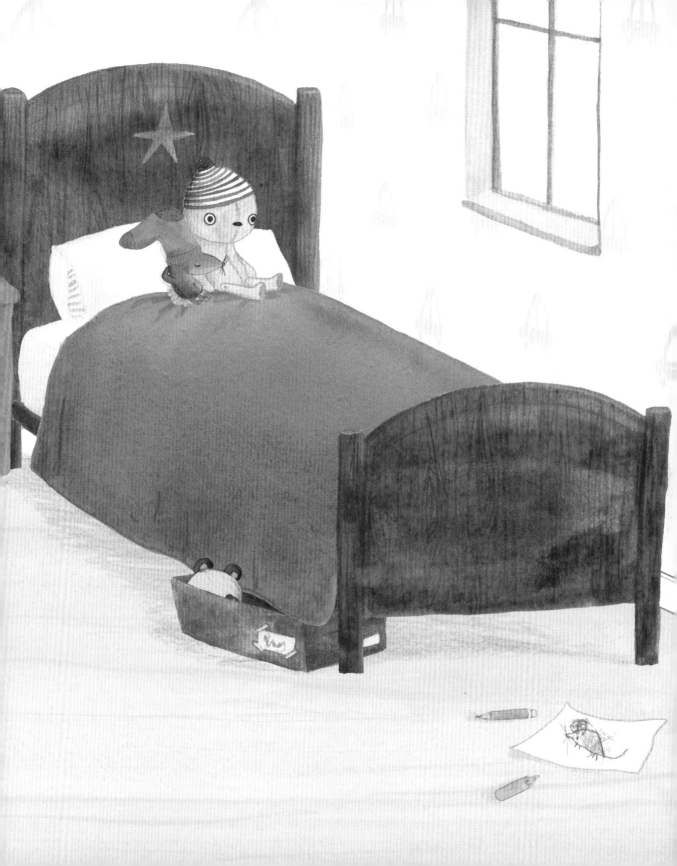

but this is not a mouse.

There are no mice in *this* house!

What's that?
A mouse has a whiskery, pointy nose ...

but this is not a mouse.

There are no mice in *this* house!

What a good mouse-scarer I am,
Clemmie thinks.
There are no mice in this house.
And she curls up for a nap.

But wait...

Crinkle!
Rustle!
Bang!

What's that?

It has a long pink tail.
It has two round ears.
It has a whiskery, pointy nose.

It's a mouse!

Clemmie has finally seen a mouse –
and it got away.

But Clemmie has learned a new trick that
might just help her catch that mouse...

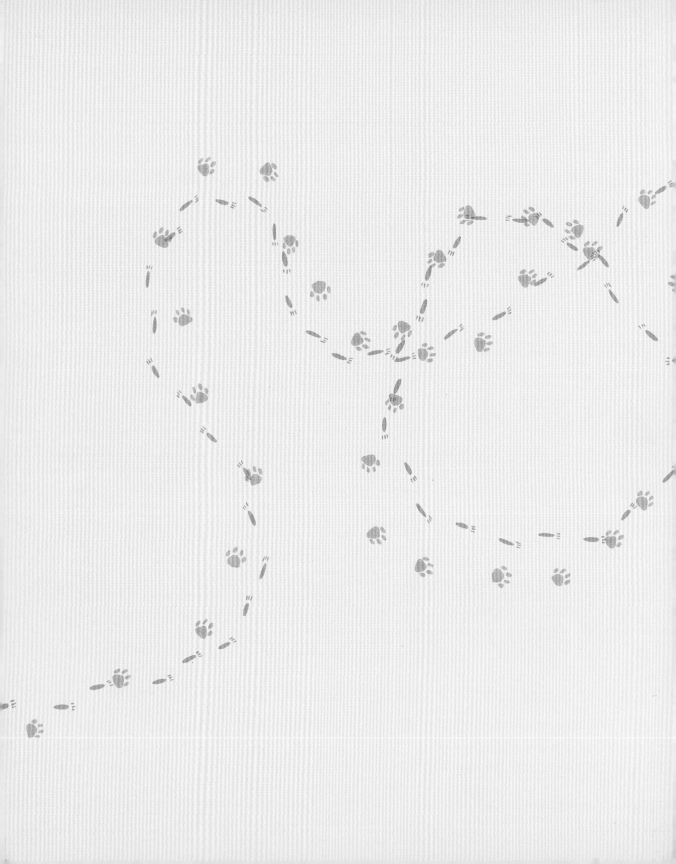